ANKY

by Laura Gates Galvin
Illustrated by Adrian Chesterman

For Kai Woods, future paleontologist...
(and firefighter and truck driver and train conductor and police officer...) — L.G.G.

For Charity, Chloe, Charlotte and Charlie from their Dino-dad — A.C.

Published by Soundprints, an imprint of Trudy Corporation, Norwalk, Connecticut.

Book design: Marcin D. Pilchowski
Book layout: Konrad Krukowski
Editor: Barbie Heit Schwaeber
Production Editor: Brian E. Giblin

First Edition 2007
10 9 8 7 6 5 4 3 2 1
Printed in China

Acknowledgments:
Our very special thanks to Dr. Matthew T. Carrano of the Smithsonian Institution's National Museum of Natural History.
Soundprints would also like to thank Ellen Nanney and Katie Mann at the Smithsonian Institution's Office of Product Development and Licensing for their help in the creation of this book.

The following books were used as reference for illustrating this title:
Gardom, Tim and Milner, Dr. Angela: *The Natural History Museum Book of Dinosaurs.* UK: Carlton Books, 2001.
Lindsay, William: *On the Trail of Incredible Dinosaurs.* New York: DK Publishers, 1998.
Man, John: *The Day of the Dinosaur.* London: Bison Books, 1978.
Norman, Dr. David: *The Illustrated Encyclopedia of Dinosaurs.* New York: Crescent Books, 1985.
Norman, Dr. David and Milner, Dr. Angela: *Eyewitness Books: Dinosaur.* New York: Knopf, 1989.
Parker, Steve and Lindsay, William: *Dinosaurs and How They Lived.* New York: DK Publishers, 1991.

A Note to the Reader: Throughout this story you will see words in *italic letters.* This is the proper scientific way to print the name of a specific dinosaur.

ANKYLOSAURUS FIGHTS BACK

by Laura Gates Galvin
Illustrated by Adrian Chesterman

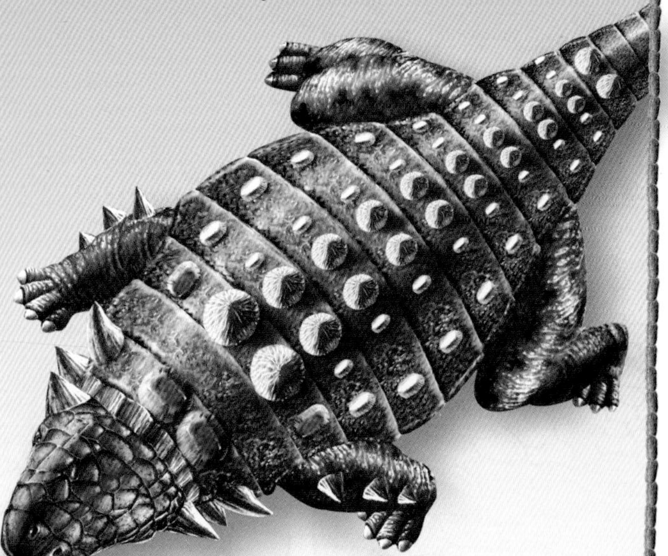

Soundprints
Where Children Discover...

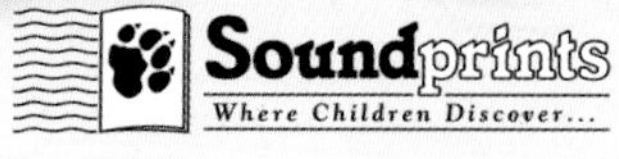

As the sun rises on a warm summer day, a *Pteranodon* soars through the sky above an ancient river. Crunching noises fill the air as a giant, tank-like dinosaur plods down to the water, crushing all the sticks and twigs in his path. It's an *Ankylosaurus* making his way to the riverbank.

At the river's edge, *Ankylosaurus* begins to chomp on plants. He is a large dinosaur with a large gut and a large appetite to match. He eats and eats and eats to satisfy his hunger.

The plants *Ankylosaurus* eats are not very nutritious, so he must consume a vast amount of them. After his snack, *Ankylosaurus's* stomach begins to churn.

At first, a low rumbling sound comes from *Ankylosaurus's* stomach, but soon the rumbling becomes louder and louder. Suddenly, *Ankylosaurus* expels a huge blast of gas! Birds fly from their nests and animals flee at the alarming sound.

Because of the food he eats, *Ankylosaurus* always has terrible gas. He even has an extra-large stomach to store it all.

Ankylosaurus is so busy eating that he doesn't know that a *Tyrannosaurus rex* is in the area. *Tyrannosaurus rex* is unfazed by *Ankylosaurus's* bad gas. *Tyrannosaurus rex* is hungry. *Ankylosaurus* would make a tasty meal!

Ankylosaurus is relieved that his stomach is settled and he can start eating again. *Ankylosaurus* peacefully chews and swallows his food until he hears a loud, crashing sound filling the air.

Ankylosaurus looks up just in time to see the huge *Tyrannosaurus rex* stomping toward him. *Ankylosaurus* might not be a smart dinosaur, but he knows when danger is near. He crouches down low and positions himself so that his tail faces the approaching *Tyrannosaurus rex*.

Ankylosaurus hears the thundering footsteps of the *Tyrannosaurus rex* coming closer and closer. Suddenly, *Tyrannosaurus rex* stops—she has found *Ankylosaurus*. The *Tyrannosaurus rex* is enormous. She towers over *Ankylosaurus*!

The *Tyrannosaurus rex* begins snapping at *Ankylosaurus*, revealing rows of huge, pointy teeth every time she opens her mouth.

The armour plates and rows of spikes that cover *Ankylosaurus* protect him from the sharp teeth of *Tyrannosaurus rex*. The only way the *Tyrannosaurus rex* can harm *Ankylosaurus* is to flip him over and expose his soft, unprotected belly.

Ankylosaurus needs to act fast! He swings his heavy tail at the *Tyrannosaurus rex*. On the second swing, the large, bony club on his tail makes contact with the larger dinosaur's leg, cracking the bone.

The *Tyrannosaurus rex* is thrown off balance and begins to sway. *Ankylosaurus* isn't very fast, but he is able to get away from the injured *Tyrannosaurus rex*!

It was a close call, but *Ankylosaurus* is safe for now. He makes his way back to the river. Anything in his path—snakes, insects or small mammals—must get out of the way quickly, or they will be trampled by *Ankylosaurus*!

All is calm back at the river. A prehistoric crocodile floats lazily across the water. The early morning sounds of chirping birds and animals splashing in the water have quieted in the midday heat.

Ankylosaurus is happy to be eating again. He tugs and chews on the low-lying plants. He eats as much of the tough vegetation as he can, until…uh oh, his stomach is unsettled again. The loud rumbling starts. And, here it comes—another thunderous blast of gas!

The silence of the peaceful river is broken, but at least *Ankylosaurus's* stomach feels better and *Ankylosaurus* can get back to eating.

ABOUT THE ANKYLOSAURUS (ang-KIE-lo-SAWR-russ)

The *Ankylosaurus* roamed the earth over 65 million years ago near the end of the Cretaceous period. The *Ankylosaurus* was 25 feet long, 6 feet wide and approximately 4 feet tall. It weighed about 5 tons! The body of *Ankylosaurus* was covered with bony plates set close together in thick, leathery skin. These plates helped protect *Ankylosaurus* from predators. The *Ankylosaurus* also had a bony club at the end of its tail that it could swing back and forth to defend itself. Bony knobs and spikes protected its head.

The *Ankylosaurus* was an herbivore, which means it only ate plants. The *Ankylosaurus* cropped large amounts of plants using its horny beak. It may have had a fermentation compartment in its very large gut to aid in digestion. Because of this compartment, the *Ankylosaurus* would have produced an enormous amount of gas!

PICTORIAL GLOSSARY

▲ ***Anatotitan***

▲ ***Triceratops***

▲ **Crocodile**

▲ ***Ankylosaurus***

▲ ***Pteranodon***

▲ ***Tyrannosaurus rex***

▲ ***Ichthyornis***

▲ ***Ornithomimos***